Maths Together

There's a lot more to maths than numbers and sums;
it's an important language which helps us describe, explore and
explain the world we live in. So the earlier children develop
an appreciation and understanding of maths, the better.

We use maths all the time – when we shop or travel from one
place to another, for example. Even when we fill the kettle we are
estimating and judging quantities. Many games and puzzles
involve maths. So too do stories and poems, often
in an imaginative and interesting way.

Maths Together is a collection of high-quality picture
books designed to introduce children, simply and enjoyably, to basic
mathematical ideas – from counting and measuring to pattern and probability.
By listening to the stories and rhymes, talking about them and asking questions,
children will gain the confidence to try out the mathematical ideas for
themselves – an important step in their numeracy development.

You don't have to be a mathematician to help your child
learn maths. Just as by reading aloud you play a vital role in
their literacy development, so by sharing the *Maths Together* books
with your child, you will play an important part in developing their
understanding of mathematics. To help you, each book has detailed
notes at the back, explaining the mathematical ideas that it
introduces, with suggestions for further related activities.

With *Maths Together*, you can count on
doing the very best for your child.

To Seth Caine, who helped me find my wings
J. D.
For Greta, my baby bird
R. A.

First published 1998 by Walker Books Ltd
87 Vauxhall Walk, London SE11 5HJ

This edition produced 2002 for
The Book People Ltd, Hall Wood Avenue,
Haydock, St Helens WA11 9UL

2 4 6 8 10 9 7 5 3 1

Text © 1998 Joyce Dunbar
Illustrations © 1998 Russell Ayto
Introductory and concluding notes © 1999 Jeannie Billington and Grace Cook

The right of Joyce Dunbar to be identified as author of this work
has been asserted by her in accordance with the Copyright, Designs and Patents Act 1988.

This book has been typeset in Gothic Blond and Fontesque.

Printed in Singapore

British Library Cataloguing in Publication Data
A catalogue record for this book is available from the British Library.

ISBN 0-7445-6627-7 (hb)
ISBN 0-7445-6603-X (pb)

Baby Bird

Written by
Joyce Dunbar

Illustrated by
Russell Ayto

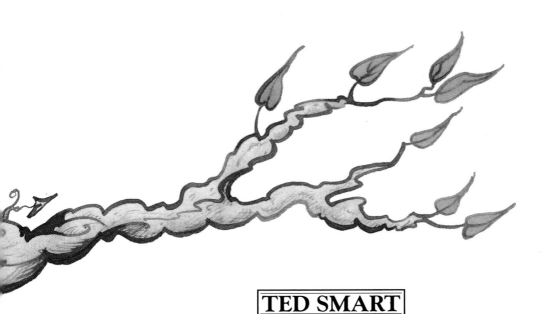

TED SMART

This is the
bird that

climbed out of the
nest and ...

flop

flop

flop   ... he fell!

This is the
squirrel that

sniffed at the
bird that fell.

This is the
bee that

buzzed round the
bird that fell.

This is the
frog that

hopped over the
bird that fell.

This is the
cat that

stalked the
bird ...

and fell
himself

(which was
just as well).

This is the dog
that opened wide

and a bird that
nearly walked inside.

A baby bird that
wanted to fly

up, up above, up above
in the sky ...

and thought he
would have

just one more
try ...

flap

flap

flap

flap

flap

flap...

This is the
bird that

flew!

About this book

The story of Baby Bird's journey from his nest
and back again gives children a gentle introduction to two
difficult mathematical concepts: position and direction.

When Baby Bird falls out of his nest, he goes on a journey
and meets some animals along the way. Each animal is in a
different position in relation to Baby Bird — for instance,
the bee buzzes round Baby Bird, the frog jumps over him.
Through reading the story together, and acting it out,
your child will get to know the meaning of
these position words.

Baby Bird meets a squirrel first, then a bee, a frog,
a cat, and a dog. When he flies back home he retraces
his route, so he sees the animals in reverse order.
Remembering the order in which things come is an
important part of knowing where you are and
developing a sense of direction.

Later on, children use this knowledge to learn more
precise ways of describing where something is (position)
and how to get to it (direction).

Notes for parents

Talking about the story together is a good way of helping children to use words which describe where something is.

You can use this picture map to trace Baby Bird's journey from his nest and back again. This helps children to follow the order in which he meets the different animals, and to retell the story in their own words.

Start →

↓

Finish ←

Every day, you and your child use words to say how to find things and where to put them.

Dad, where's my football?

Look under the stairs. It's next to the green box.

Now go under my slide.

I'm too big for this!

You could make up an obstacle course together – for each other, or for your child's toys. Take it in turns to give instructions.

Any journey – visiting friends, going shopping or to the playgroup – gives you both the chance to talk about directions.

Where do we go next?

Through the park.

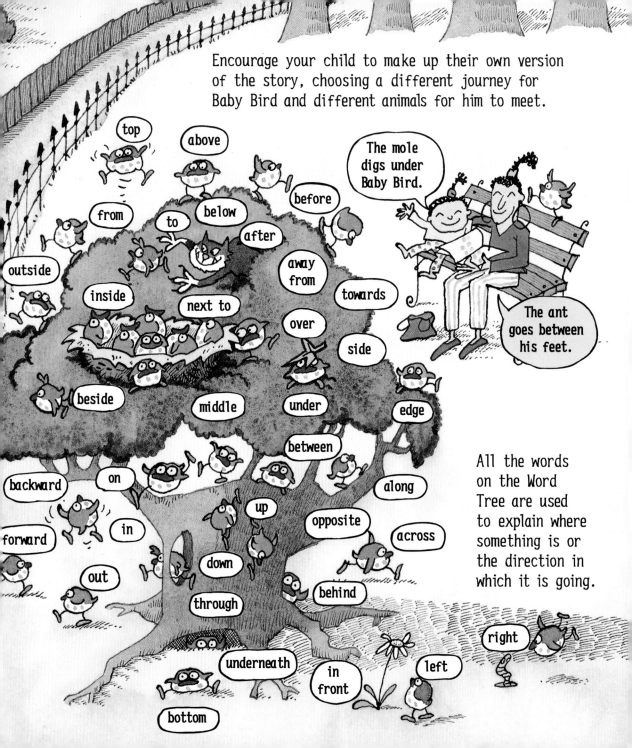

Maths Together

The *Maths Together* programme is divided into two sets – yellow (age 3+) and green (age 5+). There are six books in each set, helping children learn maths through story, rhyme, games and puzzles.

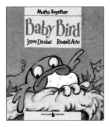

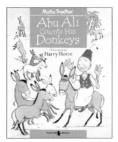